Francis Thompson

Sister-songs : An Offering to two Sisters

Francis Thompson

Sister-songs : An Offering to two Sisters

ISBN/EAN: 9783337007744

Printed in Europe, USA, Canada, Australia, Japan

Cover: Foto ©Andreas Hilbeck / pixelio.de

More available books at **www.hansebooks.com**

SISTER-SONGS
AN OFFERING TO
TWO SISTERS
BY FRANCIS THOMPSON

LONDON · JOHN LANE AT THE
BODLEY HEAD VIGO STREET
BOSTON · COPELAND AND DAY
1895

PREFACE

THIS poem, though new in the sense of being now for the first time printed, was written some four years ago, about the same date as the *Hound of Heaven* in my former volume.

One image in the *Proem* was an unconscious plagiarism from the beautiful image in Mr. Patmore's *St. Valentine's Day* :—

> " O baby Spring,
> That flutter'st sudden 'neath the breast of Earth,
> A month before the birth ! "

Finding I could not disengage it without injury to the passage in which it is embedded, I have preferred to leave it, with this acknowledgment to a Poet rich enough to lend to the poor.

FRANCIS THOMPSON.

1895.

SISTER SONGS

An Offering to Two Sisters

The Proem

SHREWD winds and shrill—were these the speech of
    May?
  A ragged, slag-grey sky—invested so,
  Mary's spoilt nursling! wert thou wont to go?
    Or *thou*, Sun-god and song-god, say
Could singer pipe one tiniest linnet-lay,
  While Song did turn away his face from song?
    Or who could be
In spirit or in body hale for long,—
  Old Æsculap's best Master!—lacking thee

At length, then, thou art here !

On the earth's lethèd ear

Thy voice of light rings out exultant, strong ;

Through dreams she stirs and murmurs at that
summons dear :

From its red leash my heart strains tamelessly,

For Spring leaps in the womb of the young year !

Nay, was it not brought forth before,

And we waited, to behold it,

Till the sun's hand should unfold it,

What the year's young bosom bore ?

Even so ; it came, nor knew we that it came,

In the sun's eclipse.

Yet the birds have plighted vows,

And from the branches pipe each other's name ;

Yet the season all the boughs

Has kindled to the finger-tips,—

Mark yonder, how the long laburnum drips

Its jocund spilth of fire, its honey of wild flame !

Yea, and myself put on swift quickening,

And answer to the presence of a sudden Spring.

From cloud-zoned pinnacles of the secret spirit

Song falls precipitant in dizzying streams;
And, like a mountain-hold when war-shouts stir it,
The mind's recessèd fastness casts to light
Its gleaming multitudes, that from every height
    Unfurl the flaming of a thousand dreams.
Now therefore, thou who bring'st the year to birth,
    Who guid'st the bare and dabbled feet of May ;
Sweet stem to that rose Christ, who from the earth
Suck'st our poor prayers, conveying them to Him ;
    Be aidant, tender Lady, to my lay !
    Of thy two maidens somewhat must I say,
Ere shadowy twilight lashes, drooping, dim
    Day's dreamy eyes from us ;
    Ere eve has struck and furled
The beamy-textured tent transpicuous,
    Of webbèd cœrule wrought and woven calms,
    Whence has paced forth the lambent-footed sun.
And Thou disclose my flower of song upcurled,
    Who from Thy fair irradiant palms
    Scatterest all love and loveliness as alms ;
    Yea, Holy One,
Who coin'st Thyself to beauty for the world !

Then, Spring's little children, your lauds do ye upraise
To Sylvia, O Sylvia, her sweet, feat ways!
　Your lovesome labours lay away,
　And trick you out in holiday,
　　For syllabling to Sylvia;
And all you birds on branches, lave your mouths with
　May,
　To bear with me this burthen,
　　For singing to Sylvia.

Part the First

THE leaves dance, the leaves sing,
The leaves dance in the breath of the Spring.
      I bid them dance,
        I bid them sing,
      For the limpid glance
        Of my ladyling ;
For the gift to the Spring of a dewier spring,
For God's good grace of this ladyling !
I know in the lane, by the hedgerow track,
    The long, broad grasses underneath
Are warted with rain like a toad's knobbed back ;
    But here May weareth a rainless wreath.
In the new-sucked milk of the sun's bosom
Is dabbled the mouth of the daisy-blossom ;
    The smouldering rosebud chars through its sheath;
The lily stirs her snowy limbs,

Ere she swims
Naked up through her cloven green,
Like the wave-born Lady of Love Hellene ;
And the scattered snowdrop exquisite
Twinkles and gleams,
As if the showers of the sunny beams
Were splashed from the earth in drops of light.
Everything
That is child of Spring
Casts its bud or blossoming
Upon the stream of my delight.

Their voices, that scents are, now let them upraise
To Sylvia, O Sylvia, her sweet, feat ways !
Their lovely mother them array,
And prank them out in holiday,
For syllabling to Sylvia ;
And all the birds on branches lave their mouths with
May,
To bear with me this burthen,
For singing to Sylvia.

2.

While thus I stood in mazes bound
    Of vernal sorcery,
I heard a dainty dubious sound,
    As of goodly melody ;
Which first was faint as if in swound,
    Then burst so suddenly
In warring concord all around,
    That, whence this thing might be,
        To see
The very marrow longed in me !
    It seemed of air, it seemed of ground,
      And never any witchery
    Drawn from pipe, or reed, or string,
    Made such dulcet ravishing.
    'Twas like no earthly instrument,
    Yet had something of them all
    In its rise, and in its fall ;
As if in one sweet consort there were blent
    Those archetypes celestial
Which our endeavouring instruments recall.

So heavenly flutes made murmurous plain
To heavenly viols, that again
—Aching with music—wailed back pain ;
Regals release their notes, which rise
Welling, like tears from heart to eyes ;
And the harp thrills with thronging sighs.
Horns in mellow flattering
Parley with the cithern-string :—
Hark !—the floating, long-drawn note
Woos the throbbing cithern-string !

Their pretty, pretty prating those citherns sure upraise
For homage unto Sylvia, her sweet, feat ways :
Those flutes do flute their vowelled lay,
Their lovely languid language say,
For lisping to Sylvia ;
Those viols' lissom bowings break the heart of May,
And harps harp their burthen,
For singing to Sylvia.

3.

Now at that music and that mirth
Rose, as 'twere, veils from earth ;

And I spied
How beside
Bud, bell, bloom, an elf
Stood, or was the flower itself
  'Mid radiant air
  All the fair
Frequence swayed in irised wavers.
Some against the gleaming rims
  Their bosoms prest
Of the kingcups, to the brims
Filled with sun, and their white limbs
Bathèd in those golden lavers ;
Some on the brown, glowing breast
Of that Indian maid, the pansy,
(Through its tenuous veils confest
Of swathing light), in a quaint fancy
Tied her knot of yellow favours ;
Others dared open draw
Snapdragon's dreadful jaw :
Some, just sprung from out the soil,
Sleeked and shook their rumpled fans
  Dropt with sheen

Of moony green ;
Others, not yet extricate,
On their hands leaned their weight.
And writhed them free with mickle toil,
Still folded in their veiny vans :
And all with an unsought accord
Sang together from the sward ;
Whence had come, and from sprites
Yet unseen, those delights,
As of tempered musics blent,
Which had given me such content.
For haply our best instrument,
Pipe or cithern, stopped or strung,
Mimics but some spirit tongue.

Their amiable voices, I bid them upraise
To Sylvia, O Sylvia, her sweet, feat ways ;
Their lovesome labours laid away,
To linger out this holiday
In syllabling to Sylvia;
While all the birds on branches lave their mouths with
May,

To bear with me this burthen,
    For singing to Sylvia.

4.

Next I saw, wonder-whist,
How from the atmosphere a mist,
So it seemed, slow uprist ;
And, looking from those elfin swarms,
        I was 'ware
        How the air
Was all populous with forms
Of the Hours, floating down,
Like Nereids through a watery town.
Some, with languors of waved arms,
Fluctuous oared their flexile way ;
Some were borne half resupine
On the aërial hyaline,
Their fluid limbs and rare array
Flickering on the wind, as quivers
Trailing weed in running rivers ;
And others, in far prospect seen,
Newly loosed on this terrene,

Shot in piercing swiftness came,
With hair a-stream like pale and goblin flame.
As crystálline ice in water,
Lay in air each faint daughter ;
Inseparate (or but separate dim)
Circumfused wind from wind-like vest,
Wind-like vest from wind-like limb.
But outward from each lucid breast,
When some passion left its haunt,
Radiate surge of colour came,
Diffusing blush-wise, palpitant,
Dying all the filmy frame.
With some sweet tenderness they would
Turn to an amber-clear and glossy gold ;
Or a fine sorrow, lovely to behold,
Would sweep them as the sun and wind's joined flood
Sweeps a greening-sapphire sea ;
Or they would glow enamouredly
Illustrious sanguine, like a grape of blood ;
Or with mantling poetry
Curd to the tincture which the opal hath,
Like rainbows thawing in a moonbeam bath.

So paled they, flushed they, swam they, sang melo-
    diously.

Their chanting, soon fading, let them, too, upraise
For homage unto Sylvia, her sweet, feat ways ;
    Weave with suave float their wavèd way,
    And colours take of holiday,
        For syllabling to Sylvia ;
And all the birds on branches lave their mouths with
    May,
    To bear with me this burthen,
        For singing to Sylvia.

5.

Then, through those translucencies,
As grew my senses clearer clear,
Did I see, and did I hear,
How under an elm's canopy
Wheeled a flight of Dryades
Murmuring measured melody.
Gyre in gyre their treading was,
Wheeling with an adverse flight,
In twi-circle o'er the grass,

These to left, and those to right ;
    All the band
Linkèd by each other's hand ;
Decked in raiment stainèd as
The blue-helmèd aconite.
And they advance with flutter, with grace,
    To the dance
Moving on with a dainty pace,
As blossoms mince it on river swells.
Over their heads their cymbals shine,
Round each ankle gleams a twine
    Of twinkling bells—
Tune twirled golden from their cells.
Every step was a tinkling sound,
As they glanced in their dancing-ground.
Clouds in cluster with such a sailing
Float o'er the light of the wasting moon,
As the cloud of their gliding veiling
Swung in the sway of the dancing-tune.
There was the clash of their cymbals clanging,
Ringing of swinging bells clinging their feet ;
And the clang on wing it seemed a-hanging,

Hovering round their dancing so fleet.—
I stirred, I rustled more than meet ;
Whereat they broke to the left and right,
With eddying robes like aconite
    Blue of helm ;
And I beheld to the foot o' the elm.

They have not tripped those dances, betrayed to my gaze,
To glad the heart of Sylvia, beholding of their maze;
    Through barky walls have slid away,
    And tricked them in their holiday,
        For other than for Sylvia ;
While all the birds on branches lave their mouths with
    May,
    And bear with me this burthen,
        For singing to Sylvia.

6.

Where its umbrage was enrooted,
    Sat white-suited,
Sat green-amiced, and bare-footed,
    Spring amid her minstrelsy ;
There she sat amid her ladies,

Where the shade is
Sheen as Enna mead ere Hades'
Gloom fell thwart Persephone.
Dewy buds were interstrown
Through her tresses hanging down,
And her feet
Were most sweet,
Tinged like sea-stars, rosied brown.
A throng of children like to flowers were sown
About the grass beside, or clomb her knee :
I looked who were that favoured company.
And one there stood
Against the beamy flood
Of sinking day, which, pouring its abundance,
Sublimed the illuminous and volute redundance
Of locks that, half dissolving, floated round her face ;
As see I might
Far off a lily-cluster poised in sun
Dispread its gracile curls of light.
I knew what chosen child was there in place !
I knew there might no brows be, save of one,
With such Hesperian fulgence compassèd,

Which in her moving seemed to wheel about her head.

O Spring's little children, more loud your lauds upraise,
For this is even Sylvia, with her sweet, feat ways!
   Your lovesome labours lay away,
   And prank you out in holiday,
    For syllabling to Sylvia;
And all you birds on branches, lave your mouths with
   May,
   To bear with me this burthen,
    For singing to Sylvia!

7.

Spring, goddess, is it thou, desirèd long?
And art thou girded round with this young train?—
If ever I did do thee ease in song,
Now of thy grace let me one meed obtain,
    And list thou to one plain.
    Oh, keep still in thy train
After the years when others therefrom fade,
    This tiny, well-belovèd maid!
To whom the gate of my heart's fortalice,
    With all which in it is,

3

And the shy self who doth therein immew him
'Gainst what loud leagurers battailously woo him,
    I, bribèd traitor to him,
    Set open for one kiss.

Then suffer, Spring, thy children, that lauds they should
    upraise
To Sylvia, this Sylvia, her sweet, feat ways ;
    Their lovely labours lay away,
    And trick them out in holiday,
      For syllabling to Sylvia ;
And that all birds on branches lave their mouths with
    May,
    To bear with me this burthen,
      For singing to Sylvia.

3.

    A kiss ? for a child's kiss ?
    Aye, goddess, even for this.
  Once, bright Sylviola ! in days not far,
Once—in that nightmare-time which still doth haunt
My dreams, a grim, unbidden visitant—
    Forlorn, and faint, and stark,

I had endured through watches of the dark
    The abashless inquisition of each star,
Yea, was the outcast mark
        Of all those heavenly passers' scrutiny ;
        Stood bound and helplessly
For Time to shoot his barbèd minutes at me ;
Suffered the trampling hoof of every hour
        In night's slow-wheelèd car ;
    Until the tardy dawn dragged me at length
    From under those dread wheels ; and, bled of
        strength,
    I waited the inevitable last.
    Then there came past
A child ; like thee, a spring-flower ; but a flower
Fallen from the budded coronal of Spring,
And through the city-streets blown withering.
She passed,—O brave, sad, lovingest, tender thing !—
And of her own scant pittance did she give,
    That I might eat and live :
Then fled, a swift and trackless fugitive.
    Therefore I kissed in thee
The heart of Childhood, so divine for me ;

And her, through what sore ways,
And what unchildish days,
Borne from me now, as then, a trackless fugitive.
Therefore I kissed in thee
Her, child ! and innocency,
And spring, and all things that have gone from me,
And that shall never be ;
All vanished hopes, and all most hopeless bliss,
Came with thee to my kiss.
And ah ! so long myself had strayed afar
From child, and woman, and the boon earth's green,
And all wherewith life's face is fair beseen ;
Journeying its journey bare
Five suns, except of the all-kissing sun
Unkissed of one ;
Almost I had forgot
The healing harms,
And whitest witchery, a-lurk in that
Authentic cestus of two girdling arms :
And I remembered not
The subtle sanctities which dart
From childish lips' unvalued precious brush,

Nor how it makes the sudden lilies push
  Between the loosening fibres of the heart.
    Then, that thy little kiss
    Should be to me all this,
Let workaday wisdom blink sage lids thereat ;
Which towers a flight three hedgerows high, poor bat !
  And straightway charts me out the empyreal air.
Its chart I wing not by, its canon of worth
Scorn not, nor reck though mine should breed it mirth:
And howso thou and I may be disjoint,
Yet still my falcon spirit makes her point
    Over the covert where
Thou, sweetest quarry, hast put in from her !

(Soul, hush these sad numbers, too sad to upraise
In hymning bright Sylvia, unlearn'd in such ways!
  Our mournful moods lay we away,
  And prank our thoughts in holiday,
    For syllabling to Sylvia ;
When all the birds on branches lave their mouths with
  May,
  To bear with us this burthen,
    For singing to Sylvia !)

9.

Then thus Spring, bounteous lady, made reply :
" O lover of me and all my progeny,
      For grace to you
I take her ever to my retinue.
Over thy form, dear child, alas ! my art
Cannot prevail ; but mine immortalising
      Touch I lay upon thy heart.
      Thy soul's fair shape
In my unfading mantle's green I drape,
And thy white mind shall rest by my devising
     A Gideon-fleece amid life's dusty drouth.
If Even burst yon globèd yellow grape
(Which is the sun to mortals' sealèd sight)
      Against her stainèd mouth ;
      Or if white-handed light
Draw thee yet dripping from the quiet pools,
      Still lucencies and cools,
Of sleep, which all night mirror constellate dreams ;
Like to the sign which led the Israelite,
      Thy soul, through day or dark,
A visible brightness on the chosen ark

Of thy sweet body and pure,

Shall it assure,

With auspice large and tutelary gleams,

Appointed solemn courts, and covenanted streams."

Cease, Spring's little children, now cease your lauds to
*   raise ;*

That dream is past, and Sylvia, with her sweet, feat
*   ways.*

*   Our lovèd labour, laid away,*

*   Is smoothly ended ; said our say,*

*   Our syllabling to Sylvia.*

Make sweet, you birds on branches ! make sweet your
*   mouths with May !*

*   But borne is this burthen,*

*   Sung unto Sylvia.*

Part the Second

AND now, thou elder nursling of the nest;
  Ere all the intertangled west
   Be one magnificence
Of multitudinous blossoms that o'errun
The flaming brazen bowl o' the burnished sun
   Which they do flower from,
How shall I 'stablish *thy* memorial?
Nay, how or with what countenance shall I come
   To plead in my defence
   For loving thee at all?
I who can scarcely speak my fellows' speech,
Love their love, or mine own love to them teach;
A bastard barred from their inheritance,
  Who seem, in this dim shape's uneasy nook,
Some sun-flower's spirit which by luckless chance
  Has mournfully its tenement mistook;

When it were better in its right abode,
Heartless and happy lackeying its god.
How com'st thou, little tender thing of white,
Whose very touch full scantly me beseems,
How com'st thou resting on my vaporous dreams,
Kindling a wraith there of earth's vernal green ?
Even so as I have seen,
In night's aërial sea with no wind blust'rous,
A ribbèd tract of cloudy malachite
Curve a shored crescent wide ;
And on its slope marge shelving to the night
The stranded moon lay quivering like a lustrous
Medusa newly washed up from the tide,
Lay in an oozy pool of its own deliquious light.

Yet hear how my excuses may prevail,
Nor, tender white orb, be thou opposite !
Life and life's beauty only hold their revels
In the abysmal ocean's luminous levels.
There, like the phantasms of a poet pale,
The exquisite marvels sail :
Clarified silver ; greens and azures frail

As if the colours sighed themselves away,
And blent in supersubtile interplay
As if they swooned into each other's arms ;
Repured vermilion,
Like ear-tips 'gainst the sun ;
And beings that, under night's swart pinion,
Make every wave upon the harbour-bars
A beaten yolk of stars.
But where day's glance turns baffled from the deeps,
Die out those lovely swarms ;
And in the immense profound no creature glides or
creeps.

Love and love's beauty only hold their revels
In life's familiar, penetrable levels :
What of its ocean-floor ?
I dwell there evermore.
From almost earliest youth
I raised the lids o' the truth,
And forced her bend on me her shrinking sight ;
Ever I knew me Beauty's eremite,
In antre of this lowly body set,

Girt with a thirsty solitude of soul,
Nathless I not forget
How I have, even as the anchorite,
I too, imperishing essences that console.
Under my ruined passions, fallen and sere,
The wild dreams stir like little radiant girls,
Whom in the moulted plumage of the year
Their comrades sweet have buried to the curls.
Yet, though their dedicated amorist,
How often do I bid my visions hist,
Deaf to them, pleading all their piteous fills ;
Who weep, as weep the maidens of the mist
Clinging the necks of the unheeding hills :
And their tears wash them lovelier than before,
That from grief's self our sad delight grows more.
Fair are the soul's uncrispèd calms, indeed,
Endiapered with many a spiritual form
Of blosmy-tinctured weed ;
But scarce itself is conscious of the store
Suckled by it, and only after storm
Casts up its loosened thoughts upon the shore.
To this end my deeps are stirred ;

And I deem well why life unshared
Was ordainèd me of yore.
In pairing-time, we know, the bird
Kindles to its deepmost splendour,
And the tender
Voice is tenderest in its throat :
Were its love, for ever nigh it,
Never by it,
It might keep a vernal note,
The crocean and amethystine
In their pristine
Lustre linger on its coat.
Therefore must my song-bower lone be,
That my tone be
Fresh with dewy pain alway ;
She, who scorns my dearest care ta'en,
An uncertain
Shadow of the sprite of May.
And is my song sweet, as they say ?
'Tis sweet for one whose voice has no reply,
Save silence's sad cry :
And are its plumes a burning bright array ?

They burn for an unincarnated eye.
A bubble, charioteered by the inward breath
    Which, ardorous for its own invisible lure,
Urges me glittering to aërial death,
    I am rapt towards that bodiless paramour ;
Blindly the uncomprehended tyranny
    Obeying of my heart's impetuous might.
        The earth and all its planetary kin,
Starry buds tangled in the whirling hair
That flames round the Phoebean wassailer,
    Speed no more ignorant, more predestined flight,
    Than I, *her* viewless tresses netted in.
As some most beautiful one, with lovely taunting,
Her eyes of guileless guile o'ercanopies,
    Does her hid visage bow,
And miserly your covetous gaze allow,
    By inchmeal, coy degrees,
    Saying—" Can you see me now ? "
Yet from the mouth's reflex you guess the wanting
    Smile of the coming eyes
In all their upturned grievous witcheries,
    Before that sunbreak rise ;

And each still hidden feature view within
Your mind, as eager scrutinies detail
The moon's young rondure through the shamefast veil
      Drawn to her gleaming chin :
        After this wise,
From the enticing smile of earth and skies
I dream my unknown Fair's refusèd gaze ;
And guessingly her love's close traits devise,
      Which she with subtile coquetries
Through little human glimpses slow displays,
        Cozening my mateless days
        By sick, intolerable delays.
And so I keep mine uncompanioned ways ;
And so my touch, to golden poesies
Turning love's bread, is bought at hunger's price.
So,—in the inextinguishable wars
  hich roll song's Orient on the sullen night
Whose ragged banners in their own despite
Take on the tinges of the hated light,—
So Sultan Phœbus has his Janizars.

But if mine unappeasèd cicatrices
        Might get them lawful ease ;
Were any gentle passion hallowed me,
    Who must none other breath of passion feel
    Save such as winnows to the fledgèd heel
        The tremulous Paradisal plumages ;
        The conscious sacramental trees
            Which ever be
            Shaken celestially,
Consentient with enamoured wings, might know my
    love for thee.

Yet is there more, whereat none guesseth, love !
    Upon the ending of my deadly night
(Whereof thou hast not the surmise, and slight
Is all that any mortal knows thereof),
    Thou wert to me that earnest of day's light,
When, like the back of a gold-mailèd saurian
    Heaving its slow length from Nilotic slime,
The first long gleaming fissure runs Aurorian
    Athwart the yet dun firmament of prime.
Stretched on the margin of the cruel sea
        Whence they had rescued me,
    With faint and painful pulses was I lying ;

Not yet discerning well
If I had 'scaped, or were an icicle,
Whose thawing is its dying.
Like one who sweats before a despot's gate,
Summoned by some presaging scroll of fate,
And knows not whether kiss or dagger wait ;
And all so sickened is his countenance,
The courtiers buzz, " Lo, doomed !" and look at him
askance :—
At Fate's dread portal then
Even so stood I, I ken,
Even so stood I, between a joy and fear,
And said to mine own heart, "Now if the end be here!"

They say, Earth's beauty seems completest
To them that on their death-beds rest ;
Gentle lady ! she smiles sweetest
Just ere she clasp us to her breast.
And I,—now *my* Earth's countenance grew bright,
Did she but smile me towards that nuptial-night ?
But, whileas on such dubious bed I lay,
One unforgotten day,
As a sick child waking sees

Wide-eyed daisies
Gazing on it from its hand,
Slipped there for its dear amazes ;
So between thy father's knees
I saw *thee* stand,
And through my hazes
Of pain and fear thine eyes' young wonder shone.
Then, as flies scatter from a carrion,
Or rooks in spreading gyres like broken smoke
Wheel, when some sound their quietude has broke,
Fled, at thy countenance, all that doubting spawn :
The heart which I had questioned spoke,
A cry impetuous from its depths was drawn,—
" I take the omen of this face of dawn ! "
And with the omen to my heart cam'st thou.
Even with a spray of tears
That one light draft was fixed there for the years.

And now ?—
The hours I tread ooze memories of thee, Sweet !
Beneath my casual feet.
With rainfall as the lea,

The day is drenched with thee ;
In little exquisite surprises
Bubbling deliciousness of thee arises
From sudden places,
Under the common traces
Of my most lethargied and customed paces.

As an Arab journeyeth
Through a sand of Ayaman,
Lean Thirst, lolling its cracked tongue,
Lagging by his side along ;
And a rusty-wingèd Death
Grating its low flight before,
Casting ribbèd shadows o'er
The blank desert, blank and tan :
He lifts by hap toward where the morning's roots are
His weary stare,—
Sees, although they plashless mutes are,
Set in a silver air
Fountains of gelid shoots are,
Making the daylight fairest fair ;
Sees the palm and tamarind

Tangle the tresses of a phantom wind ;—
A sight like innocence when one has sinned !
A green and maiden freshness smiling there,
　　　While with unblinking glare
The tawny-hided desert crouches watching her.

　　　'Tis a vision :
　　Yet the greeneries Elysian
　　He has known in tracts afar ;
　　Thus the enamouring fountains flow,
　　Those the very palms that grow,
By rare-gummed Sava, or Herbalimar.—

　　Such a watered dream has tarried
　　Trembling on my desert arid ;
　　　　Even so
　　　Its lovely gleamings
　　　　Seemings show
　　Of things not seemings ;
　　　　And I gaze,
　　Knowing that, beyond my ways,
　　　　Verily

All these *are*, for these are she.
Eve no gentlier lays her cooling cheek
On the burning brow of the sick earth,
    Sick with death, and sick with birth,
Aeon to aeon, in secular fever twirled,
      Than thy shadow soothes this weak
      And distempered being of mine.
In all I work, my hand includeth thine ;
      Thou rushest down in every stream
Whose passion frets my spirit's deepening gorge ;
Unhood'st mine eyas-heart, and fliest my dream ;
      Thou swing'st the hammers of my forge ;
As the innocent moon, that nothing does but shine,
Moves all the labouring surges of the world.
    Pierce where thou wilt the springing thought
      in me,
And there thy pictured countenance lies enfurled,
    As in the cut fern lies the imaged tree.
      This poor song that sings of thee,
    This fragile song, is but a curled
      Shell outgathered from thy sea,
And murmurous still of its nativity.

Princess of Smiles!
Sorceress of most unlawful-lawful wiles!
Cunning pit for gazers' senses,
Overstrewn with innocences!
Purities gleam white like statues
In the fair lakes of thine eyes,
And I watch the sparkles that use
There to rise,
Knowing these
Are bubbles from the calyces
Of the lovely thoughts that breathe
Paving, like water-flowers, thy spirit's floor beneath.

O thou most dear!
Who art thy sex's complex harmony
God-set more facilely;
To thee may love draw near
Without one blame or fear,
Unchidden save by his humility:
Thou Perseus' Shield! wherein I view secure
The mirrored Woman's fateful-fair allure!
Whom Heaven still leaves a twofold dignity,

As girlhood gentle, and as boyhood free ;
With whom no most diaphanous webs enwind
The barèd limbs of the rebukeless mind.
Wild Dryad ! all unconscious of thy tree,
       With which indissolubly
The tyrannous time shall one day make thee whole ;
Whose frank arms pass unfretted through its bole :
     Who wear'st thy femineity
Light as entrailèd blossoms, that shalt find
It erelong silver shackles unto thee.
Thou whose young sex is yet but in thy soul ;—
     As hoarded in the vine
Hang the gold skins of undelirious wine,
As air sleeps, till it toss its limbs in breeze :—
   In whom the mystery which lures and sunders,
     Grapples and thrusts apart ; endears, estranges ;
—The dragon to its own Hesperides—
   Is gated under slow-revolving changes,
Manifold doors of heavy-hingèd years.
    So once, ere Heaven's eyes were filled with wonders
      To see Laughter rise from Tears,

Lay in beauty not yet mighty,
　　Conchèd in translucencies,
　The antenatal Aphrodite,
Caved magically under magic seas ;
Caved dreamlessly beneath the dreamful seas.

　　" Whose sex is in thy soul ! "
　　What think we of thy soul ?
　Which has no parts, and cannot grow,
　　Unfurled not from an embryo ;
Born of full stature, lineal to control ;
　And yet a pigmy's yoke must undergo.
Yet must keep pace and tarry, patient, kind,
With its unwilling scholar, the dull, tardy mind ;
Must be obsequious to the body's powers,
Whose low hands mete its paths, set ope and close its
　　ways ;
　　Must do obeisance to the days,
And wait the little pleasure of the hours ;
　　Yea, ripe for kingship, yet must be
Captive in statuted minority !
So is all power fulfilled, as soul in thee.

So still the ruler by the ruled takes rule,
And wisdom weaves itself i' the loom o' the fool.
The splendent sun no splendour can display,
Till on gross things he dash his broken ray,
From cloud and tree and flower re-tossed in prismy
  spray.
Did not obstruction's vessel hem it in,
Force were not force, would spill itself in vain ;
We know the Titan by his champèd chain.
Stay is heat's cradle, it is rocked therein,
And by check's hand is burnished into light ;
If hate were none, would love burn lowlier bright ?
God's Fair were guessed scarce but for opposite sin ;
Yea, and His Mercy, I do think it well,
Is flashed back from the brazen gates of Hell.
   The heavens decree
All power fulfil itself as soul in thee.
For supreme Spirit subject was to clay,
  And Law from its own servants learned a law,
And Light besought a lamp unto its way,
   And Awe was reined in awe,
   At one small house of Nazareth ;

And Golgotha
Saw Breath to breathlessness resign its breath,
And Life do homage for its crown to death.

So is all power, as soul in thee increased !
　　But, knowing this, in knowledge's despite
　　I fret against the law severe that stains
　　　　Thy spirit with eclipse ;
　　When—as a nymph's carven head sweet water
　　　　drips,
　　For others oozing so the cool delight
　　Which cannot steep her stiffened mouth of stone—
Thy nescient lips repeat maternal strains.
　　　　Memnonian lips !
Smitten with singing from thy mother's east,
　　And murmurous with music not their own :
　　Nay, the lips flexile, while the mind alone
　　　　A passionless statue stands.
　　　　Oh, pardon, innocent one !
　　Pardon at thine unconscious hands !
" Murmurous with music not their own," I say ?
And in that saying how do I missay,

When from the common sands
Of poorest common speech of common day
Thine accents sift the golden musics out !
And ah, we poets, I misdoubt,
Are little more than thou !
We speak a lesson taught we know not how,
And what it is that from us flows
The hearer better than the utterer knows.

Thou canst foreshape thy word ;
The poet is not lord
Of the next syllable may come
With the returning pendulum ;
And what he plans to-day in song,
To-morrow sings it in another tongue.
Where the last leaf fell from his bough,
He knows not if a leaf shall grow,
Where he sows he doth not reap,
He reapeth where he did not sow ;
He sleeps, and dreams forsake his sleep
To meet him on his waking way.
Vision will mate him not by law and vow :

Disguised in life's most hodden-grey,
By the most beaten road of everyday
She waits him, unsuspected and unknown.
　　　The hardest pang whereon
He lays his mutinous head may be a Jacob's stone.
In the most iron crag his foot can tread
　　　A Dream may strew her bed,
　　　And suddenly his limbs entwine,
And draw him down through rock as sea-nymphs
　　　might through brine.
But, unlike those feigned temptress-ladies who
In guerdon of a night the lover slew,
When the embrace has failed, the rapture fled,
Not he, not he, the wild sweet witch is dead !
　　　And, though he cherisheth
The babe most strangely born from out her death,
Some tender trick of her it hath, maybe,—
　　　It is not she !

Yet, even as the air is rumorous of fray
　　　Before the first shafts of the sun's onslaught
　　　　From gloom's black harness splinter,

And Summer move on Winter
With the trumpet of the March, and the pennon of the
    May ;
      As gesture outstrips thought ;
So, haply, toyer with ethereal strings !
Are thy blind repetitions of high things
The murmurous gnats whose aimless hoverings
    Reveal song's summer in the air ;
The outstretched hand, which cannot thought declare,
      Yet is thought's harbinger.
These strains the way for thine own strains prepare ;
We feel the music moist upon this breeze,
And hope the congregating poesies.
    Sundered yet by thee from us
    Wait, with wild eyes luminous,
All thy winged things that are to be ;
They flit against thee, Gate of Ivory !
They clamour on the portress Destiny,—
" Set her wide, so we may issue through !
Our vans are quick for that they have to do."
    Suffer still your young desire ;
Your plumes but bicker at the tips with fire,

Tarry their kindling ; they will beat the higher.
And thou, bright girl, not long shalt thou repeat
Idly the music from thy mother caught ;
      Not vainly has she wrought,
Not vainly from the cloudward-jetting turret
Of her aërial mind, for thy weak feet,
Let down the silken ladder of her thought.
    She bare thee with a double pain,
      Of the body and the spirit ;
    Thou thy fleshly weeds hast ta'en,
      Thy diviner weeds inherit!
The precious streams which through thy young lips roll
Shall leave their lovely delta in thy soul :
    Where sprites of so essential kind
      Set their paces,
    Surely they shall leave behind
      The green traces
Of their sportance in the mind ;
And thou shalt, ere we well may know it,
    Turn that daintiness, a poet,—
      Elfin-ring
    Where sweet fancies foot and sing.

So it may be, so it *shall* be,—
Oh, take the prophecy from me !
What if the old fastidious sculptor, Time,
This crescent marvel of his hands
Carveth all too painfully,
And I who prophesy shall never see ?
What if the niche of its predestined rhyme,
Its aching niche, too long expectant stands ?
Yet shall he after sore delays
On some exultant day of days
The white enshrouding childhood raise
From thy fair spirit, finished for our gaze ;
While we (but 'mongst that happy " we "
The prophet cannot be !)
While we behold with no astonishments,
With that serene fulfilment of delight
Wherewith we view the sight
When the stars pitch the golden tents
Of their high campment on the plains of night.
Why should amazement be our satellite ?
What wonder in such things ?
If angels have hereditary wings,

If not by Salic law is handed down
　　The poet's crown,
To thee, born in the purple of the throne,
　　The laurel must belong :
　　Thou, in thy mother's right.
Descendant of Castalian-chrismed kings—
　　O Princess of the Blood of Song !

Peace ; too impetuously have I been winging
　　Toward vaporous heights which beckon and beguile :
　　I sink back, saddened to my inmost mind ;
Even as I list a-dream that mother singing
　　The poesy of sweet tone, and sadden, while
　　Her voice is cast in troubled wake behind
　　The keel of her keen spirit.　Thou art enshrined
In a too primal innocence for this eye—
Intent on such untempered radiancy—
Not to be pained ; my clay can scarce endure
Ungrieved the effluence near of essences so pure.
　　Therefore, little, tender maiden,
　　Never be thou overshaden
　　With a mind whose canopy

Would shut out the sky from thee ;
Whose tangled branches intercept Heaven's light :
I will not feed my unpastured heart
On thee, green pleasaunce as thou art,
To lessen by one flower thy happy daisies white.
The water-rat is earth-hued like the runlet
Whereon he swims ; and how in me should lurk
Thoughts apt to neighbour thine, thou creature sunlit ?
If through long fret and irk
Thine eyes within their browed recesses were
Worn caves where thought lay couchant in its lair ;
Wert thou a spark among dank leaves, ah ruth !
With age in all thy veins, while all thy heart was
    youth ;
Our contact might run smooth.
But life's Eoan dews still moist thy ringèd hair ;
Dian's chill finger-tips
Thaw if at night they happen on thy lips ;
The flying fringes of the sun's cloak frush
The fragile leaves which on those warm lips blush ;
And joy only lurks retirèd
In the dim gloaming of thine irid.

Then since my love drags this poor shadow, me,
And one without the other may not be,
      From both I guard thee free.
    It still is much, yes, it is much,
Only—my dream!—to love my love of thee ;
     And it is much, yes, it is much,
In hands which thou hast touched to feel thy touch,
In voices which have mingled with thine own
      To hear a double tone.
As anguish, for supreme expression prest,
     Borrows its saddest tongue from jest,
     Thou hast of absence so create
     A presence more importunate ;
     And thy voice pleads its sweetest suit
      When it is mute.
     I thank the once accursèd star
      Which did me teach
To make of Silence my familiar,
Who hath the rich reversion of thy speech,
Since the most charming sounds thy thought can wear,
Cast off, fall to that pale attendant's share ;
     And thank the gift which made my mind

5

A shadow-world, wherethrough the shadows wind
Of all the loved and lovely of my kind.

Like a maiden Saxon, folden,
     As she flits, in moon-drenched mist ;
Whose curls streaming flaxen-golden,
     By the misted moonbeams kist,
Dispread their filmy floating silk
     Like honey steeped in milk :
So, vague goldenness remote,
     Through my thoughts I watch thee float.
When the snake summer casts her blazoned skin
We find it at the turn of autumn's path,
And think it summer that rewinded hath,
          Joying therein ;
And this enamouring slough of thee, mine elf,
          I take it for thyself;
Content.   Content ?   Yea, title it content.
The very loves that belt thee must prevent
My love, I know, with their legitimacy :
As the metallic vapours, that are swept
Athwart the sun, in his light intercept

The very hues
Which *their* conflagrant elements effuse.
But, my love, my heart, my fair,
That only I should see thee rare,
Or tent to the hid core thy rarity,—
This were a mournfulness more piercing far
Than that those other loves my own must bar,
Or thine for others leave thee none for me.

But on a day whereof I think,
One shall dip his hand to drink
In that still water of thy soul,
And its imaged tremors race
Over thy joy-troubled face,
As the intervolved reflections roll
From a shaken fountain's brink,
With swift light wrinkling its alcove.
From the hovering wing of Love
The warm stain shall flit roseal on thy cheek.
Then, sweet blushet! whenas he,
The destined paramount of thy universe,
Who has no worlds to sigh for, ruling thee,

Ascends his vermeil throne of empery,
      One grace alone I seek.
Oh! may this treasure-galleon of my verse,
Fraught with its golden passion, oared with cadent
    rhyme,
Set with a towering press of fantasies,
      Drop safely down the time,
    Leaving mine islèd self behind it far
Soon to be sunken in the abysm of seas,
(As down the years the splendour voyages
    From some long ruined and night-submergèd star),
And in thy subject sovereign's havening heart
Anchor the freightage of its virgin ore;
      Adding its wasteful more
To his own overflowing treasury.
So through his river mine shall reach thy sea,
      Bearing its confluent part;
      In his pulse mine shall thrill;
And the quick heart shall quicken from the heart
    that's still.

Ah! help, my Dæmon that hast served me well!

Not at this last, oh, do not me disgrace!
I faint, I sicken, darkens all my sight,
As, poised upon this unprevisioned height,
    I lift into its place
The utmost aery traceried pinnacle.
So; it is builded, the high tenement,
    —God grant—to mine intent!
Most like a palace of the Occident,
    Up-thrusting, toppling maze on maze,
    Its mounded blaze,
And washèd by the sunset's rosy waves,
Whose sea drinks rarer hue from those rare walls it
    laves.
    Yet wail, my spirits, wail!
So few therein to enter shall prevail!
Scarce fewer could win way, if their desire
A dragon baulked, with involuted spire,
And writhen snout spattered with yeasty fire.
For at the elfin portal hangs a horn
    Which none can wind aright
    Save the appointed knight
Whose lids the fay-wings brushed when he was born.

All others stray forlorn,
Or glimpsing, through the blazoned windows scrolled
Receding labyrinths lessening tortuously
    In half obscurity ;
With mystic images, inhuman, cold,
      That flameless torches hold.
    But who can wind that horn of might
(The horn of dead Heliades) aright,—
        Straight
Open for him shall roll the conscious gate ;
And light leap up from all the torches there,
And life leap up in every torchbearer,
And the stone faces kindle in the glow,
And into the blank eyes the irids grow,
And through the dawning irids ambushed meanings
    show.
    Illumined this wise on,
He threads securely the far intricacies,
    With brede from Heaven's wrought vesture over-
    strewn ;
Swift Tellus' purfled tunic, girt upon
With the blown chlamys of her fluttering seas ;

And the freaked kirtle of the pearlèd moon :
Until he gain the structure's core, where stands—
    A toil of magic hands—
The unbodied spirit of the sorcerer,
        Most strangely rare,
    As is a vision remembered in the noon ;
Unbodied, yet to mortal seeing clear,
Like sighs exhaled in eager atmosphere.
From human haps and mutabilities
It rests exempt, beneath the edifice
        To which itself gave rise ;
Sustaining centre to the bubble of stone
Which, breathed from it, exists by it alone.
Yea, ere Saturnian earth her child consumes,
    And I lie down with outworn ossuaries,
Ere death's grim tongue anticipates the tomb's
        Siste viator, in this storied urn
        My living heart is laid to throb and burn,
    Till end be ended, and till ceasing cease.

And thou by whom this strain hath parentage ;
    Wantoner between the yet untreacherous claws

Of newly-whelped existence ! ere he pause,
What gift to thee can yield the archimage ?
     For coming seasons' frets
     What aids, what amulets,
     What softenings, or what brightenings ?
As Thunder writhes the lash of his long lightnings
    About the growling heads of the brute main
    Foaming at mouth, until it wallow again
    In the scooped oozes of its bed of pain ;
So all the gnashing jaws, the leaping heads
Of hungry menaces, and of ravening dreads,
      Of pangs
Twitch-lipped, with quivering nostrils and immitigate
    fangs,
I scourge beneath the torment of my charms
That their repentless nature fear to work thee harms.
And as yon Apollonian harp-player,
     Yon wandering psalterist of the sky,
With flickering strings which scatter melody,
The silver-stolèd damsels of the sea,
     Or lake, or fount, or stream,
    Enchants from their ancestral heaven of waters

To Naiad it through the unfrothing air;
      My song enchants so out of undulous dream
    The glimmering shapes of its dim-tressèd daugh-
        ters,
And missions each to be thy minister.
      Saying; " O ye,
The organ-stops of being's harmony;
The blushes on existence's pale face,
      Lending it sudden grace;
Without whom we should but guess Heaven's worth
By blank negations of this sordid earth,
      (So haply to the blind may light
Be but gloom's undetermined opposite);
Ye who are thus as the refracting air
Whereby we see Heaven's sun before it rise
Above the dull line of our mortal skies;
As breathing on the strainèd ear that sighs
From comrades viewless unto strainèd eyes,
Soothing our terrors in the lampless night;
Ye who can make this world where all is deeming
What world ye list, being arbiters of seeming;
Attend upon her ways, benignant powers!

Unroll ye life a carpet for her feet,
And cast ye down before them blossomy hours,
Until her going shall be clogged with sweet!
All dear emotions whose new-bathèd hair,
Still streaming from the soul, in love's warm air
Smokes with a mist of tender fantasies ;
                    All these,
And all the heart's wild growths which, swiftly bright,
Spring up the crimson agarics of a night,
No pain in withering, yet a joy arisen ;
And all thin shapes more exquisitely rare,
                    More subtly fair,
Than these weak ministering words have spell to prison
Within the magic circle of this rhyme ;
And all the fays who in our creedless clime
                    Have sadly ceased
Bearing to other children childhood's proper feast ;
Whose robes are fluent crystal, crocus-hued,
        Whose wings are wind a-fire, whose mantles
            wrought
            From spray that falling rainbows shake
                to air;

These, ye familiars to my wizard thought,
Make things of journal custom unto her ;
With lucent feet imbrued,
If young Day tread, a glorious vintager,
The wine-press of the purple-foamèd east ;
Or round the nodding sun, flush-faced and sunken,
His wild bacchantes drunken
Reel, with rent woofs a-flaunt, their westering rout.
—But lo ! at length the day is lingered out,
At length my Ariel lays his viol by ;
We sing no more to thee, child, he and I ;
The day is lingered out :
In slow wreaths folden
Around yon censer, spherèd, golden,
Vague Vesper's fumes aspire ;
And glimmering to eclipse
The long laburnum drips
Its honey of wild flame, its jocund spilth of fire.

Now pass your ways, fair bird, and pass your ways,
If you will ;

I have you through the days !
And flit or hold you still,
And perch you where you list
 On what wrist,—
You are mine through the times !
I have caught you fast for ever in a tangle of sweet
 rhymes.

 And in your young maiden morn,
  You may scorn,
  But you must be
 Bound and sociate to me ;
With this thread from out the tomb my dead hand shall
 tether thee !

Go, sister-songs, to that sweet sister-pair
For whom I have your frail limbs fashionèd,
 And framèd feateously ;—
For whom I have your frail limbs fashionèd
With how great shamefastness and how great dread,

Knowing you frail, but not if you be fair,
> Though framèd feateously ;
> Go unto them from me.
Go from my shadow to their sunshine sight,
> Made for all sights' delight ;
Go like twin swans that oar the surgy storms
To bate with pennoned snows in candent air :
> Nigh with abasèd head,
Yourselves linked sisterly, that sister-pair,
> And go in presence there ;
Saying—"Your young eyes cannot see our forms,
Nor read the yearning of our looks aright ;
But time shall trail the veilings from our hair,
And cleanse your seeing with his euphrasy,
(Yea, even your bright seeing make more bright,
> Which is all sights' delight),
And ye shall know us for what things we be.

"Whilom, within a poet's calyxed heart,
A dewy love we trembled all apart ;
> Whence it took rise
> Beneath your radiant eyes,

Which misted it to music.   We must long,
A floating haze of silver subtile song,
      Await love-laden
      Above each maiden
The appointed hour that o'er the hearts of you—
      As vapours into dew
      Unweave, whence they were wove,—
Shall turn our loosening musics back to love."

Inscription

WHEN the last stir of bubbling melodies
Broke as my chants sank underneath the wave
Of dulcitude, but sank again to rise
Where man's embaying mind those waters lave,
(For music hath its Oceanides
Flexuously floating through their parent seas,
      And such are these),
I saw a vision—or may it be
The effluence of a dear desired reality?
      I saw two spirits high,—
Two spirits, dim within the silver smoke
      Which is for ever woke
By snowing lights of fountained Poesy.
Two shapes they were familiar as love ;
      They were those souls, whereof
One twines from finest gracious daily things,
Strong, constant, noticeless, as are heart-strings,

The golden cage wherein this song-bird sings ;
And the other's sun gives hue to all my flowers,
Which else pale flowers of Tartarus would grow,
Where ghosts watch ghosts of blooms in ghostly
        bowers ;—
                For we do know
The hidden player by his harmonics,
And by my thoughts I know what still hands thrill
        the keys.

And to these twain—as from the mind's abysses
All thoughts draw toward the awakening heart's sweet
        kisses,
With proffer of their wreathen fantasies,—
            Even so to these
I saw how many brought their garlands fair,
Whether of song, or simple love, they were,—
Of simple love, that makes best garlands fair.
But one I marked who lingered still behind,
As for such souls no seemly gift had he :
            He was not of their strain,
Nor worthy of so bright beings to entertain,

Nor fit compeer for such high company.
Yet was he, surely, born to them in mind,
Their youngest nursling of the spirit's kind.
              Last stole this one,
With timid glance, of watching eyes adread,
And dropped his frightened flower when all were gone;
And where the frail flower fell, it withered.
But yet methought those high souls smiled thereon ;
As when a child, upstraining at your knees
Some fond and fancied nothings, says, " I give you
        these ! "

Poems

BY

FRANCIS THOMPSON

With Frontispiece, Title-page, and Cover Design by
LAURENCE HOUSMAN

Fourth Edition, pott 4to, 5s. net

"A new poet, and this time a major and not a minor one. . . . Swinburne, William Morris, George Meredith, among the elder of our present-day poets, William Watson and Norman Gale among the juniors, have each their poetical genius, or something approaching it ; but here is another to add to the small band."—*St. James's Gazette.*

"They are written, to borrow a phrase of Chaucer's, in the 'high style'; their harmonies are at times almost Miltonic, and yet original in cadence. . . . The most promising work by a young poet which has seen the light for a long time."—*Guardian.*

"I can hardly doubt that at least that minority who can recognise the essentials under the accidents of poetry, and who feel that it is to poetic Form only and not to forms that eternity belongs, will agree that, alike in wealth and dignity of imagination, in depth and subtlety of thought, and in magic and mastery of language, a new poet of the first rank is to be welcomed in the author of this volume."—MR. H. D. TRAILL in *Nineteenth Century.*

"Profound thought and far-fetched splendour of imagery, and nimble-witted discernment of those analogies which are the 'roots' of the poet's language, abound . . . qualities which ought to place him, even should he do no more than he has done, in the prominent ranks of fame, with Cowley and Crashaw."—MR. COVENTRY PATMORE in *Fortnightly Review.*

"There is enough and more remaining to prove that in this work there is a power of thought, of imagination, and of language which must give pause to every reader inclined to believe that high verse is dead and done with."—*Pall Mall Gazette.*

"They are the most fascinating poems which have appeared since Rossetti."—*Daily Chronicle.*

" Mr. Francis Thompson is endowed with very precious gifts, and we may well look to him to enrich the treasury of our poetical wealth."—*Weekly Sun.*

" Mr. Thompson's poetry attains a sublimity unsurpassed by any Victorian poet."—*Speaker.*

" He has great splendour of imagination, extraordinary fecundity of phrase, a rich vocabulary, an impassioned utterance."—*Irish Independent.*

" The thought these poems clothe is too intense, too deep, too fervent to be appreciated by the casual reader ; but every lover of poetry, proud of the richness of our English tongue, will feel indebted to Mr. Thompson for a new revelation of its beauties."— *World.*

" Those who have not merely ears, but ' ears to hear ' great poetry, will agree that the publication of this volume marks an era in English literature."—*Merrie England.*

" So remarkable a use of metaphor, and a style so entirely distinguished, are considerable capital on which to begin a poetic career."—*Star.*

" They all display the same fine bloom of young imagination."—*Scotsman.*

" If we would find sincerity, splendour of imagination, extraordinary tenderness and depth of thought, a piercing conscience of an inner life, not of much joy and of very great pain, and majesty of expression, we know not where to look among modern poets rather than to Mr. Francis Thompson."— *Tablet.*

" His very excesses are those of luxuriance, and the root of the matter is certainly there since there is so much to prune away in the blossom. Most versifiers might wish that in this respect they had half his complaint."—*Daily News.*

" We have hopes that are not cheap for his Muse's future."—*National Observer.*

" In a word, a new planet has swum into the ken of the watchers of the poetic skies. These are big words ; but we have weighed them."—*Newcastle Daily Chronicle.*

" I do not know who Mr. Francis Thompson may be ; but if the little volume which contains his ' Poems,' does not include some of the best verse which has been written for ten years, then I give up any claim to know what good poetry is."—*Queen.*

" A finely extravagant courtliness, which belongs to an older school of verse. Mr. Thompson has grappled with splendid subjects splendidly."—*Athenæum.*

" The book is one which every lover of the Muse must needs possess. It has individuality and charm, and where these are there is permanence of fame."—*Globe.*

" Francis Thompson keeps the best traditions of the Elizabethans unlowered."—*Illustrated London News.*

List of Books

IN

Belles Lettres

All the Books in this Catalogue
are Published at Net Prices

1895

Telegraphic Address
Bodleian, London

List of Books

IN

BELLES LETTRES

(Including some Transfers)

Published by John Lane

𝕿𝖍𝖊 𝕭𝖔𝖉𝖑𝖊𝖞 𝕳𝖊𝖆𝖉

Vigo Street, London, W.

N.B.—The Authors and Publisher reserve the right of reprinting any book in this list if a new edition is called for, except in cases where a stipulation has been made to the contrary, and of printing a separate edition of any of the books for America irrespective of the numbers to which the English editions are limited. The numbers mentioned do not include copies sent to the public libraries, nor those sent for review.

Most of the books are published simultaneously in England and America, and in many instances the names of the American publishers are appended.

ADAMS (FRANCIS).

ESSAYS IN MODERNITY. Cr. 8vo. 5s. net. [*Shortly.*
Chicago: Stone & Kimball.

A CHILD OF THE AGE. (*See* KEYNOTES SERIES.)

ALLEN (GRANT).

THE LOWER SLOPES : A Volume of Verse. With title-page and cover design by J. ILLINGWORTH KAY. 600 copies, cr. 8vo. 5s. net.

Chicago: Stone & Kimball.

THE WOMAN WHO DID. (*See* KEYNOTES SERIES.)

BEARDSLEY (AUBREY).

THE STORY OF VENUS AND TANNHÄUSER, in which is set forth an exact account of the Manner of State held by Madam Venus, Goddess and Meretrix, under the famous Hörselberg, and containing the adventures of Tannhäuser in that place, his repentance, his journeying to Rome, and return to the loving mountain. By AUBREY BEARDSLEY. With 20 full-page illustrations, numerous ornaments, and a cover from the same hand. Sq. 16mo. 10s. 6d. net.
[*In preparation.*

BEDDOES (T. L.).

See GOSSE (EDMUND).

BEECHING (Rev. H. C.).

IN A GARDEN : Poems. With title-page and cover design by ROGER FRY. Cr. 8vo. 5s. net.

New York: Macmillan & Co.

BENSON (ARTHUR CHRISTOPHER).

LYRICS. Fcap. 8vo, buckram. 5s. net.

New York: Macmillan & Co.

BROTHERTON (MARY).

ROSEMARY FOR REMEMBRANCE. With title-page and cover design by WALTER WEST. Fcap. 8vo. 3s. 6d. net.

CAMPBELL (GERALD).

THE JONESES AND THE ASTERISKS. With six illustrations and title-page by F. H. TOWNSEND. Fcap. 8vo. 3s. 6d. net.

New York : The Merriam Co.

CASTLE (Mrs. EGERTON).

MY LITTLE LADY ANNE: A Romance. Sq. 16mo. 2s. 6d. net.
[*In preparation.*

Philadelphia: Henry Altemus.

CASTLE (EGERTON).
See STEVENSON (ROBERT LOUIS).

CROSS (VICTORIA).
CONSUMMATION : A Novel. Cr. 8vo. 4s. 6d. net.
[*In preparation.*

DALMON (C. W.).
SONG FAVOURS. With a specially designed title-page. Sq.
16mo. 3s. 6d. net. [*In preparation.*
Chicago: Way & Williams.

D'ARCY (ELLA).
MONOCHROMES. (See KEYNOTES SERIES.)

DAVIDSON (JOHN).
PLAYS : An Unhistorical Pastoral ; A Romantic Farce ;
Bruce, a Chronicle Play ; Smith, a Tragic Farce ; Scara-
mouch in Naxos, a Pantomime. With a frontispiece and
cover design by AUBREY BEARDSLEY. Printed at the
Ballantyne Press. 500 copies, sm. 4to. 7s. 6d. net.
Chicago: Stone & Kimball.

FLEET STREET ECLOGUES. Fcap. 8vo, buckram. 5s. net.
[*Out of print at present.*

A RANDOM ITINERARY AND A BALLAD. With a frontispiece
and title-page by LAURENCE HOUSMAN. 600 copies.
Fcap. 8vo, Irish Linen. 5s. net.
Boston : Copeland & Day.

BALLADS AND SONGS. With title-page designed by WALTER
WEST. Fourth Edition. Fcap. 8vo, buckram. 5s. net.
Boston : Copeland & Day.

DAWE (W. CARLTON).
YELLOW AND WHITE. (See KEYNOTES SERIES.)

DE TABLEY (LORD).
POEMS, DRAMATIC AND LYRICAL. By JOHN LEICESTER
WARREN (Lord De Tabley). Illustrations and cover design
by C. S. RICKETTS. 2nd edition, cr. 8vo. 7s. 6d. net.
New York: Macmillan & Co.

DE TABLEY (LORD).
POEMS, DRAMATIC AND LYRICAL. 2nd series. uniform in binding with the former volume. Cr. 8vo. 5s. net.
New York: Macmillan & Co.

DIX (GERTRUDE).
THE GIRL FROM THE FARM. (*See* KEYNOTES SERIES.)

DOSTOIEVSKY (F.).
(*See* KEYNOTES SERIES, Vol. III.)

ECHEGARAY (JOSÉ).
See LYNCH (HANNAH).

EGERTON (GEORGE).
KEYNOTES. (*See* KEYNOTES SERIES.)

DISCORDS. (*See* KEYNOTES SERIES.)

YOUNG OFEG'S DITTIES. A translation from the Swedish of OLA HANSSON. Cr. 8vo. 3s. 6d. net.
Boston: Roberts Bros.

FARR (FLORENCE).
THE DANCING FAUN. (*See* KEYNOTES SERIES.)

FLETCHER (J. S.).
THE WONDERFUL WAPENTAKE. By "A SON OF THE SOIL." With 18 full-page illustrations by J. A. SYMINGTON. Cr. 8vo. 5s. 6d. net.
Chicago: A. C. McClurg & Co.

GALE (NORMAN).
ORCHARD SONGS. With title-page and cover design by J. ILLINGWORTH KAY. Fcap. 8vo. Irish Linen. 5s. net.
Also a special edition limited in number on hand-made paper bound in English vellum. £1 1s. net.
New York: G. P. Putnam's Sons.

GARNETT (RICHARD).
POEMS. With title-page by J. ILLINGWORTH KAY. 350 copies, cr. 8vo. 5s. net.
Boston: Copeland & Day.

DANTE, PETRARCH, CAMOENS. CXXIV Sonnets rendered in English. Cr. 8vo. 5s. net. [*In preparation.*

GEARY (NEVILL).
A LAWYER'S WIFE : A Novel. Cr. 8vo. 4s. 6d. net.
[*In preparation.*

GOSSE (EDMUND).
THE LETTERS OF THOMAS LOVELL BEDDOES. Now first edited. Pott 8vo. 5s. net.
Also 25 copies large paper. 12s. 6d. net.
New York: Macmillan & Co.

GRAHAME (KENNETH).
PAGAN PAPERS : A VOLUME OF ESSAYS. With title-page by AUBREY BEARDSLEY. Fcap. 8vo. 5s. net.
Chicago: Stone & Kimball.

THE GOLDEN AGE. Cr. 8vo. 3s. 6d. net.
Chicago : Stone & Kimball.

GREENE (G. A.).
ITALIAN LYRISTS OF TO-DAY. Translations in the original metres from about 35 living Italian poets with bibliographical and biographical notes. Cr. 8vo. 5s. net.
New York : Macmillan & Co.

GREENWOOD (FREDERICK).
IMAGINATION IN DREAMS. Crown 8vo. 5s. net.
New York: Macmillan & Co.

HAKE (T. GORDON).
A SELECTION FROM HIS POEMS. Edited by Mrs. MEYNELL. With a portrait after D. G. ROSSETTI, and a cover design by GLEESON WHITE. Cr. 8vo. 5s. net.
Chicago: Stone & Kimball.

HANSSON (LAURA MARHOLM).

MODERN WOMEN : Six Psychological Sketches.   [SOPHIA KOVALEVSKY, GEORGE EGERTON, ELEONORA DUSE, AMALIE SKRAM, MARIE BASHKIRTSEFF, A. EDGREN LEFFLER.] Translated from the German by HERMIONE RAMSDEN.   Cr. 8vo.   3s. 6d. net.   [*In preparation.*

HANSSON (OLA).

See EGERTON.

HARLAND (HENRY).

GREY ROSES.   (*See* KEYNOTES SERIES.)

HAYES (ALFRED).

THE VALE OF ARDEN, AND OTHER POEMS.   With a title-page and cover design by E. H. NEW.   Fcap. 8vo.   3s. 6d. net.

Also 25 copies large paper.   15s. net.

HEINEMANN (WILLIAM).

THE FIRST STEP : A Dramatic Moment.   Sm. 4to, 3s. 6d. net.

HOPPER (NORA).

BALLADS IN PROSE.   With a title-page and cover by WALTER WEST.   Sq. 16mo.   5s. net.
Boston : Roberts Bros.

HOUSMAN (LAURENCE).

GREEN ARRAS : Poems.   With illustrations by the Author.   Cr. 8vo.   5s. net.   [*In preparation.*

IRVING (LAURENCE).

GODEFROI AND YOLANDE : A Play.   With 3 illustrations by AUBREY BEARDSLEY.   Sm. 4to.   5s. net.
        [*In preparation.*

JAMES (W. P.).

ROMANTIC PROFESSIONS : A volume of Essays.   With title-page designed by J. ILLINGWORTH KAY.   Cr. 8vo.   5s. net.
New York : Macmillan & Co.

JOHNSON (LIONEL).

THE ART OF THOMAS HARDY. Six Essays, with etched portrait by WM. STRANG, and Bibliography by JOHN LANE. Second edition, cr. 8vo. Buckram. 5s. 6d. net. Also 150 copies, large paper, with proofs of the portrait. £1s. 1s. net.

New York: Dodd, Mead & Co.

JOHNSON (PAULINE).

THE WHITE WAMPUM: Poems. With title-page and cover designs by E. H. NEW. Cr. 8vo. 5s. net.

Boston: Lamson, Wolffe & Co.

JOHNSTONE (C. E.).

BALLADS OF BOY AND BEAK. Sq. 32mo. 2s. 6d. net.
[In preparation.

KEYNOTES SERIES.

Each volume with specially designed title-page by AUBREY BEARDSLEY. Cr. 8vo, cloth. 3s. 6d. net.

Vol. I. KEYNOTES. By GEORGE EGERTON.
[Seventh edition now ready.

Vol. II. THE DANCING FAUN. By FLORENCE FARR.

Vol. III. POOR FOLK. Translated from the Russian of F. DOSTOIEVSKY by LENA MILMAN, with a preface by GEORGE MOORE.

Vol. IV. A CHILD OF THE AGE. By FRANCIS ADAMS.

Vol. V. THE GREAT GOD PAN AND THE INMOST LIGHT. By ARTHUR MACHEN.
[Second edition now ready.

Vol. VI. DISCORDS. By GEORGE EGERTON.
[Fourth edition now ready.

Vol. VII. PRINCE ZALESKI. By M. P. SHIEL.

Vol. VIII. THE WOMAN WHO DID. By GRANT ALLEN.
[Fifteenth edition now ready.

Vol. IX. WOMEN'S TRAGEDIES. By H. D. LOWRY.

Vol. X. GREY ROSES. By HENRY HARLAND.

Vol. XI. AT THE FIRST CORNER, AND OTHER STORIES. By H. B. MARRIOTT WATSON.

Vol. XII. MONOCHROMES. By ELLA D'ARCY.

Vol. XIII. AT THE RELTON ARMS. By EVELYN SHARP.

KEYNOTES SERIES.

> Vol. XIV. THE GIRL FROM THE FARM. By GERTRUDE
> DIX.
>
> Vol. XV. THE MIRROR OF MUSIC. By STANLEY V.
> MAKOWER.
>
> Vol. XVI. YELLOW AND WHITE. By W. CARLTON DAWE.
>
> Vol. XVII. THE MOUNTAIN LOVERS. By FIONA MACLEOD.
>
> Vol. XVIII. THE THREE IMPOSTORS. By ARTHUR MACHEN.
>
> *Boston : Roberts Bros.*   [*In preparation.*

LANDER (HARRY).

> WEIGHED IN THE BALANCE : A Novel. Cr. 8vo. 4s. 6d. net.
>   [*In preparation.*

LANG (ANDREW).

> *See* STODDART.

LEATHER (R. K.).

> VERSES. 250 copies, fcap. 8vo. 3s. net.
>
> *Transferred by the Author to the present Publisher.*

LE GALLIENNE (RICHARD).

> PROSE FANCIES. With portrait of the Author by WILSON
> STEER. Fourth edition, cr. 8vo, purple cloth. 5s. net.
> Also a limited large paper edition. 12s. 6d. net.
> *New York : G. P. Putnam's Sons.*
>
> THE BOOK BILLS OF NARCISSUS. An account rendered by
> RICHARD LE GALLIENNE. Third edition, with a new
> chapter and a frontispiece, cr. 8vo, purple cloth. 3s. 6d.
> net.
> Also 50 copies on large paper. 8vo. 10s. 6d. net.
> *New York : G. P. Putnam's Sons.*
>
> ENGLISH POEMS. Fourth edition, revised, cr. 8vo, purple cloth.
> 4s. 6d. net.
> *Boston : Copeland & Day.*
>
> GEORGE MEREDITH: some Characteristics; with a Biblio-
> graphy (much enlarged) by JOHN LANE, portrait, &c.
> Fourth edition, cr. 8vo, purple cloth. 5s. 6d. net.

LE GALLIENNE (RICHARD).

THE RELIGION OF A LITERARY MAN. 5th thousand, cr. 8vo, purple cloth. 3s. 6d. net.

Also a special rubricated edition on band-made paper, 8vo. 10s. 6d. net.

New York: G. P. Putnam's Sons.

ROBERT LOUIS STEVENSON: An Elegy, and Other Poems, mainly personal. With etched title-page by D. Y. CAMERON. Cr. 8vo, purple cloth. 4s. 6d. net.

Also 75 copies on large paper. 8vo. 12s. 6d. net.

Boston: Copeland & Day.

RETROSPECTIVE REVIEWS: A Literary Log, 1891-1895. 2 vols., cr. 8vo, purple cloth. 7s. net.   [*In preparation.*

New York: Dodd, Mead & Co.

LOWRY (H. D.).

WOMEN'S TRAGEDIES. (*See* KEYNOTES SERIES.)

LUCAS (WINIFRED).

A VOLUME OF POEMS. Fcap. 8vo. 4s. 6d. net.
    [*In preparation.*

LYNCH (HANNAH).

THE GREAT GALEOTO AND FOLLY OR SAINTLINESS. Two Plays, from the Spanish of JOSÉ ECHEGARAY, with an Introduction. Sm. 4to. 5s. 6d. net.

Boston: Lamson, Wolffe & Co.

MACHEN (ARTHUR).

THE GREAT GOD PAN. (*See* KEYNOTES SERIES.)

THE THREE IMPOSTORS. (*See* KEYNOTES SERIES.)

MACLEOD (FIONA).

THE MOUNTAIN LOVERS. (*See* KEYNOTES SERIES.)

MAKOWER (STANLEY V.).

THE MIRROR OF MUSIC. (*See* KEYNOTES SERIES.)

MARZIALS (THEO.).

THE GALLERY OF PIGEONS, AND OTHER POEMS. Post 8vo. 4s. 6d. net.   [*Very few remain.*

Transferred by the Author to the present Publisher.

MATHEW (FRANK).

THE WOOD OF THE BRAMBLES : A Novel. Cr. 8vo. 4s. 6d.
net. [*In preparation.*

MEREDITH (GEORGE).

THE FIRST PUBLISHED PORTRAIT OF THIS AUTHOR, engraved
on the wood by W. BISCOMBE GARDNER, after the painting
by G. F. WATTS. Proof copies on Japanese vellum,
signed by painter and engraver. £1 1s. net.

MEYNELL (MRS.), (ALICE C. THOMPSON).

POEMS. Fcap. 8vo. 3s. 6d. net. (*Out of print at present.*) A
few of the 50 large paper copies (1st edition) remain.
12s. 6d. net.

THE RHYTHM OF LIFE, AND OTHER ESSAYS. 2nd edition,
fcap. 8vo. 3s. 6d. net. A few of the 50 large paper copies
(1st edition) remain, 12s. 6d. net.
See also HAKE.

MILLER (JOAQUIN).

THE BUILDING OF THE CITY BEAUTIFUL. Fcap. 8vo.
With a decorated cover. 5s. net.
Chicago: Stone & Kimball.

MILMAN (LENA).

DOSTOIEVSKY'S POOR FOLK. (*See* KEYNOTES SERIES.)

MONKHOUSE (ALLAN).

BOOKS AND PLAYS : A VOLUME OF ESSAYS ON MEREDITH,
BORROW, IBSEN AND OTHERS. 400 copies, crown 8vo.
5s. net.
Philadelphia: J. B. Lippincott Co.

MOORE (GEORGE).

(*See* KEYNOTES SERIES, Vol. III.)

NESBIT (E.).

A POMANDER OF VERSE. With a title-page and cover designed
by LAURENCE HOUSMAN. Cr. 8vo. 5s. net.
Chicago: A. C. McClurg & Co. [*In preparation.*

NETTLESHIP (J. T.).
ROBERT BROWNING. Essays and Thoughts. Third edition,
with a portrait, cr. 8vo. 5*s*. 6*d*. *net*.
New York: Chas. Scribner's Sons.

NOBLE (JAS. ASHCROFT).
THE SONNET IN ENGLAND, AND OTHER ESSAYS. Title-page
and cover design by AUSTIN YOUNG. 600 copies, cr. 8vo.
5*s*. *net*. Also 50 copies, large paper, 12*s*. 6*d*. *net*.

O'SHAUGHNESSY (ARTHUR).
HIS LIFE AND HIS WORK. With selections from his Poems.
By LOUISE CHANDLER MOULTON. Portrait and cover
design, fcap. 8vo. 5*s*. *net*.
Chicago: Stone & Kimball.

OXFORD CHARACTERS.
A series of lithographed portraits by WILL ROTHENSTEIN, with
text by F. YORK POWELL and others. To be issued monthly
in term. Each number will contain two portraits. Parts I.
to VI. ready. 200 sets only, folio, wrapper, 5*s*. *net* per part;
25 special large paper sets containing proof impressions of
the portraits signed by the artist, 10*s*. 6*d*. *net* per part.

PETERS (WM. THEODORE).
POSIES OUT OF RINGS. Sq. 16mo. 3*s*. 6*d*. *net*.
[In preparation.

PLARR (VICTOR).
IN THE DORIAN MOOD: Poems. Cr. 8vo. 5*s*. *net*.
[In preparation.

RADFORD (DOLLIE).
SONGS, AND OTHER VERSES. With title-page designed by
PATTEN WILSON. Fcap. 8vo. 4*s*. 6*d*. *net*.
Philadelphia: J. B. Lippincott Co.

RAMSDEN (HERMIONE).
See HANSSON.

RICKETTS (C. S.) AND C. H. SHANNON.
HERO AND LEANDER. By CHRISTOPHER MARLOWE and
GEORGE CHAPMAN. With borders, initials, and illus-
trations designed and engraved on the wood by C. S.
RICKETTS and C. H. SHANNON. Bound in English
vellum and gold. 200 copies only. 35*s*. *net*.
Boston: Copeland & Day.

RHYS (ERNEST).
> A LONDON ROSE, AND OTHER RHYMES. With title-page designed by SELWYN IMAGE. 350 copies, cr. 8vo. 5s. net.
> New York: Dodd, Mead & Co.

ROBINSON (C. NEWTON).
> THE VIOL OF LOVE. With ornaments and cover design by LAURENCE HOUSMAN. Cr. 8vo. 5s. net.
> Boston: Lamson, Wolffe & Co.

ST. CYRES (LORD).
> THE LITTLE FLOWERS OF ST. FRANCIS. A new rendering into English of the FIORETTI DI SAN FRANCESCO. Cr. 8vo. 5s. net.   [In preparation.

SHARP (EVELYN).
> AT THE RELTON ARMS. (See KEYNOTES SERIES.)

SHIEL (M. P.).
> PRINCE ZALESKI. (See KEYNOTES SERIES.)

STACPOOLE (H. DE VERE).
> DEATH, THE KNIGHT, AND THE LADY. Sq. 16mo. 2s. 6d. net.   [In preparation.
> Philadelphia: Henry Altemus.

STEVENSON (ROBERT LOUIS).
> PRINCE OTTO: A Rendering in French by EGERTON CASTLE. Cr. 8vo. 5s. net.   [In preparation.
> Also 100 copies on large paper, uniform in size with the Edinburgh Edition of the works.

STODDART (THOMAS TOD).
> THE DEATH WAKE. With an introduction by ANDREW LANG. Fcap. 8vo. 5s. net.
> Chicago: Way & Williams.

STREET (G. S.).
> THE AUTOBIOGRAPHY OF A BOY. Passages selected by his friend, G. S. S. With title-page designed by C. W. FURSE. Fcap. 8vo. 3s. 6d. net.
> New York: The Merriam Co.   [Fourth edition now ready.

> MINIATURES AND MOODS. Fcap. 8vo. 3s. net.
> Transferred by the Author to the present Publisher.
> New York: The Merriam Co.

SWETTENHAM (F. A.).
> MALAY SKETCHES. With title and cover designs by PATTEN
> WILSON. Cr. 8vo. 5s. net.
> *New York: Macmillan & Co.*

TABB (JOHN B.).
> POEMS. Sq. 32mo. 4s. 6d. net.
> *Boston: Copeland & Day.*

TENNYSON (FREDERICK).
> POEMS OF THE DAY AND YEAR. Cr. 8vo. 5s. net.
>   [*In preparation.*

THIMM (C. A.).
> A COMPLETE BIBLIOGRAPHY OF THE ART OF FENCE,
> DUELLING, &c. With illustrations.   [*In preparation.*

THOMPSON (FRANCIS).
> POEMS. With frontispiece, title-page, and cover design by
> LAURENCE HOUSMAN. Fourth edition, pott 4to. 5s. net.
> *Boston: Copeland & Day.*
>
> SISTER-SONGS: An Offering to Two Sisters. With frontis-
> piece, title-page, and cover design by LAURENCE HOUS-
> MAN. Pott 4to, buckram. 5s. net.
> *Boston: Copeland & Day.*

TYNAN HINKSON (KATHARINE).
> CUCKOO SONGS. With title-page and cover design by LAUR-
> ENCE HOUSMAN. Fcap. 8vo. 5s. net.
> *Boston: Copeland & Day.*
>
> MIRACLE PLAYS.   [*In preparation.*

WATSON (ROSAMUND MARRIOTT).
> VESPERTILIA, AND OTHER POEMS. With title-page designed
> by R. ANNING BELL. Fcap. 8vo. 4s. 6d. net.
>   [*In preparation.*

WATSON (H. B. MARRIOTT).
> AT THE FIRST CORNER. (*See* KEYNOTES SERIES.)

WATSON (WILLIAM).
> ODES, AND OTHER POEMS. Fourth Edition. Fcap. 8vo.
> 4s. 6d. net.
> *New York: Macmillan & Co.*

WATSON (WILLIAM).

THE ELOPING ANGELS : A CAPRICE. Second edition, sq.
16mo, buckram.   3s. 6d. net.
New York : Macmillan & Co.

EXCURSIONS IN CRITICISM ; BEING SOME PROSE RECREATIONS
OF A RHYMER.   Second edition, cr. 8vo.   5s. net.
New York : Macmillan & Co.

THE PRINCE'S QUEST, AND OTHER POEMS.   With a biblio-
graphical note added.   Second edition, fcap. 8vo.   4s. 6d.
net.

WATT (FRANCIS).

THE LAW'S LUMBER ROOM.   Fcap. 8vo.   3s. 6d. net.
                                        [*In preparation.*

WATTS (THEODORE).

POEMS.   Crown 8vo.   5s. net.   [*In preparation.*

There will also be an Edition de Luxe *of this volume, printed
at the Kelmscott Press.*

WELLS (H. G.).

SELECT CONVERSATIONS WITH AN UNCLE, NOW EXTINCT.
With a title-page designed by F. H. TOWNSEND.   Fcap.
8vo.   3s. 6d. net.
New York : The Merriam Co.

WHARTON (H. T.).

SAPPHO.   Memoir, text, selected renderings, and a literal trans-
lation by HENRY THORNTON WHARTON.   With Three
Illustrations in photogravure and a cover design by AUBREY
BEARDSLEY.   Fcap. 8vo.   7s. 6d. net.
Chicago : A. C. McClurg & Co.

The Yellow Book

An Illustrated Quarterly.   Pott 4to, 5s. net.

Volume I. April 1894, 272 pp., 15 Illustrations.

Volume II. July 1894, 364 pp., 23 Illustrations.

Volume III. October 1894, 280 pp., 15 Illustrations.

Volume IV. January 1895, 285 pp., 16 Illustrations.

Volume V.   April 1895, 317 pp., 14 Illustrations.

Boston : Copeland & Day.